PRO FOOTBALL'S UNDERDOGS:

PLAYERS AND TEAMS WHO SHOCKED THE FOOTBALL WORLD

BY MICHAEL BRADLEY

Sports Illustrated KIDS

CAPSTONE PRESS
a capstone imprint

Sports Illustrated Kids Sports Shockers! are published by Capstone Press,
1710 Roe Crest Drive, North Mankato, Minnesota 56003
www.mycapstone.com

Copyright © 2018 by Capstone Press, a Capstone imprint. All rights reserved.
No part of this publication may be reproduced in whole or in part, or stored in a
retrieval system, or transmitted in any form or by any means, electronic, mechanical,
photocopying, recording, or otherwise, without written permission of the publisher.

Sports Illustrated Kids is a trademark of Time Inc. Used with permission.

Library of Congress Cataloging-in-Publication
Names: Bradley, Michael, 1962- author.
Title: Pro Football's Underdogs : Players and Teams Who Shocked the Football World
/ by Michael Bradley
Description: North Mankato, Minnesota : Capstone Press, 2017. | Series: Sports
Illustrated Kids. Sports Shockers! | Includes index. Identifiers: LCCN 2017004669 |
ISBN 9781515780489 (library binding) | ISBN 9781515780526 (ebook)
Subjects: LCSH: Football—United States—History—Juvenile literature. | Football
players—United States—Biography—Juvenile literature.
Classification: LCC GV950.7 B72 2017 | DDC 796.332/64--dc23
LC record available at https://lccn.loc.gov/2017004669

Editorial Credits
Nick Healy, editor; Kyle Grenz, designer; Eric Gohl, media researcher;
Kathy McColley, production specialist

Photo Credits
AP Photo: Pro Football Hall of Fame, 15 (top); Getty Images: Bettmann, 14, 15
(bottom), Focus on Sport, 7 (bottom), 8, 9, 28, 29, Jamie Squire, 18, Wally McNamee, 22;
iStockphoto: OSTILL, cover (right); Newscom: KRT/Mark Reis, 19 (top), UPI/Matthew
Healey, 11 (bottom); Shutterstock: ostill, cover (left); Sports Illustrated: Al Tielemans,
10, 20, Bill Frakes, 13 (bottom), Bob Rosato, 6, 21 (all), Damian Strohmeyer, 5, 7 (top),
26, 27 (top), Heinz Kluetmeier, 4, 17 (bottom), John G. Zimmerman, 23, John Iacono, 19
(bottom), 30, John W. McDonough, 11 (top), 12, 13 (top), Peter Read Miller, 16, 17 (top),
24, Robert Beck, 31, Simon Bruty, 25, 27 (bottom)

Printed and bound in the USA.
010364F17

Table of Contents

Football's Underdogs 4
Perfect Upset 6
The Guarantee 8
Call Him "Incredelman" 10
From the Hardwood to the Gridiron 12
The Sneakers Game 14
Ugly Winners 16
Second Time's a Charm 18
Sweet Revenge 20
Johnny U. 22
Supermarket to Super Bowl 24
The Afterthought 26
Ending an Era in Style 28
Underdog Roundup 30

    Read More 32
    Internet Sites 32
    Index 32

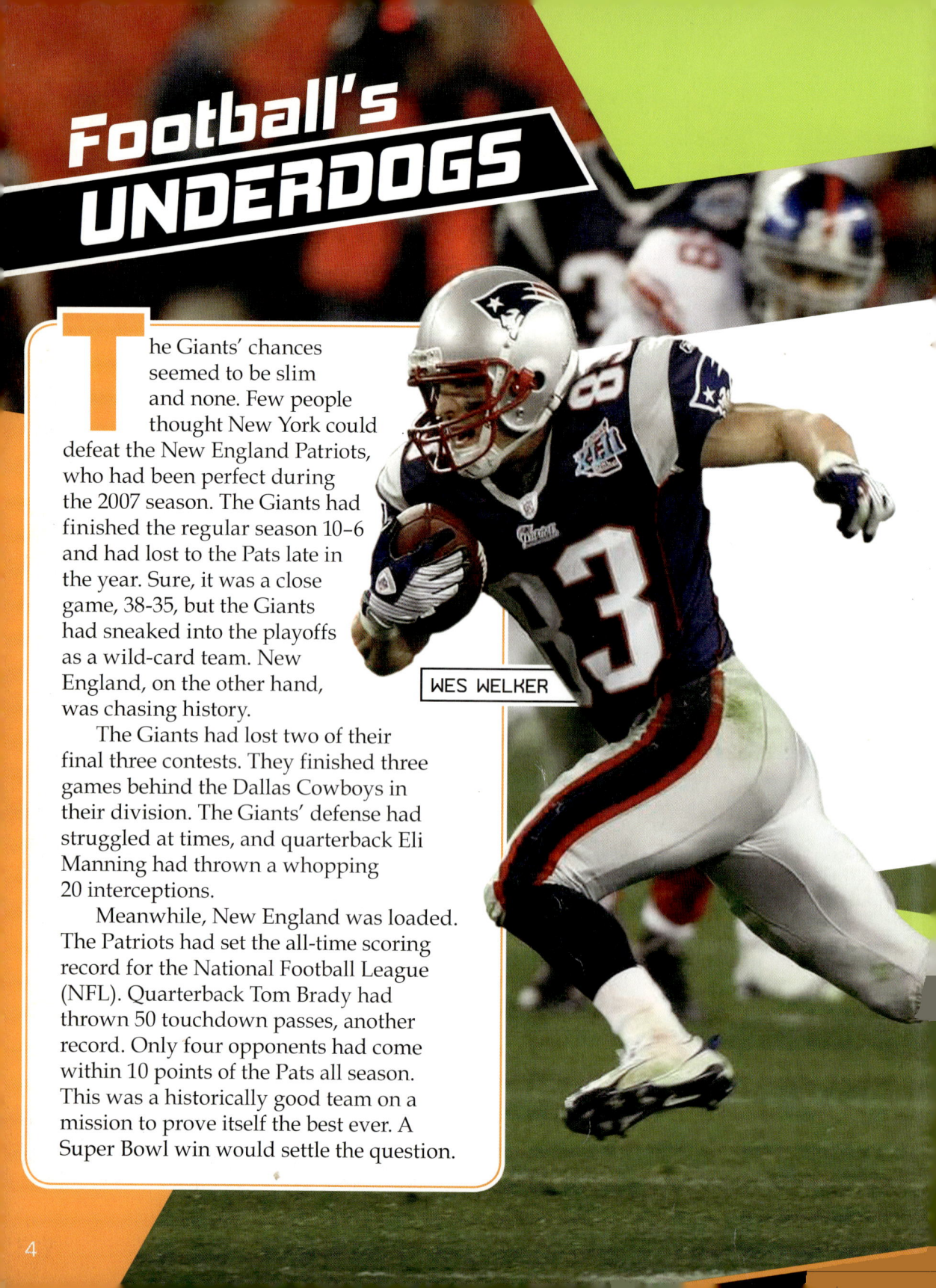

Football's UNDERDOGS

The Giants' chances seemed to be slim and none. Few people thought New York could defeat the New England Patriots, who had been perfect during the 2007 season. The Giants had finished the regular season 10–6 and had lost to the Pats late in the year. Sure, it was a close game, 38-35, but the Giants had sneaked into the playoffs as a wild-card team. New England, on the other hand, was chasing history.

The Giants had lost two of their final three contests. They finished three games behind the Dallas Cowboys in their division. The Giants' defense had struggled at times, and quarterback Eli Manning had thrown a whopping 20 interceptions.

Meanwhile, New England was loaded. The Patriots had set the all-time scoring record for the National Football League (NFL). Quarterback Tom Brady had thrown 50 touchdown passes, another record. Only four opponents had come within 10 points of the Pats all season. This was a historically good team on a mission to prove itself the best ever. A Super Bowl win would settle the question.

WES WELKER

But the Giants hung in with the mighty Patriots. At halftime, New York trailed by just four. And the Giants took a 10-7 fourth-quarter lead on a touchdown pass from Manning to David Tyree. The Patriots answered to make it 14-10.

COULD THE GIANTS COME BACK AND SPOIL THE PATS' UNDEFEATED SEASON?

A victory in Super Bowl XLII would let the Giants join some of the most amazing underdogs in NFL history.

COULD THEY PULL OFF THE ULTIMATE SURPRISE?

DAVID TYREE OF THE GIANTS SCORES AGAINST THE MIGHTY PATRIOTS.

Perfect UPSET

In 1972 the Miami Dolphins finished the season 17–0 and won Super Bowl VII. Every season since, that team's players and coaches celebrate when the last of the NFL's undefeated teams loses a game. Sometimes that has taken only six or seven weeks. Other seasons, it has taken longer.

But in 2007 the Dolphins' record was in trouble. The Patriots finished the regular season 16–0. They captured their two playoff games to enter Super Bowl XLII perfect. The Patriots were favored by two touchdowns over the Giants. After finishing the season 10–6, New York had to win three playoff games on the road to reach the big game.

QUARTERBACK ELI MANNING DODGED THE PATS' PASS RUSH AND FIRED TWO TD PASSES.

The Pats had defeated the Giants, 38-35, in the final regular season game, but the Giants entered the Super Bowl confident. The Giants' defense, which had struggled during the regular season, toughened up during the playoffs.

The Patriots had averaged 36.8 points per game that season, which was a new record. But the Giants held them to just two touchdowns in a stunning 17-14 victory.

Giants quarterback Eli Manning threw for 255 yards and two touchdowns. Defensive end Justin Tuck had two sacks as part of a ferocious New York pass rush. Late in the game, receiver David Tyree made an amazing catch by pinning the football to his helmet to keep a key late drive alive.

TYREE MAKES HIS FAMOUS HELMET CATCH.

THE GIANTS HAD RUINED NEW ENGLAND'S PERFECTION AND MADE SOME OLD DOLPHINS PRETTY DARN HAPPY.

FACT: THE 1972 DOLPHINS FINISHED THEIR PERFECT SEASON BY DEFEATING THE WASHINGTON REDSKINS IN SUPER BOWL VII. THE FINAL SCORE WAS 14-7. THE REDSKINS' POINTS CAME ON A BOTCHED FIELD-GOAL ATTEMPT LATE IN THE GAME.

POWER RUNNER LARRY CSONKA LED THE DOLPHINS.

The GUARANTEE

He was "Broadway Joe," the perfect symbol for the wild American Football League (AFL), which loved high-scoring games. New York Jets quarterback Joe Namath had led his team to Super Bowl III, where it would meet the powerful Baltimore Colts. The Colts had finished the 1968 regular season 13–1 and had pounded the Cleveland Browns in the NFL championship game, 34-0.

AT THE TIME, THE NFL AND AFL WERE SEPARATE LEAGUES. THEIR CHAMPS MET IN THE SUPER BOWL, A TRADITION THAT HAD ONLY JUST BEGUN.

The NFL still looked at the Jets and the whole AFL as something like a little brother. In the first two Super Bowls, the Green Bay Packers had beaten the Kansas City Chiefs and the Oakland Raiders handily. The Colts were 18-point favorites over the Jets.

JOE NAMATH

FACT:
THE TWO PRO FOOTBALL LEAGUES MERGED BEFORE THE 1970 SEASON. THEY FORMED TWO CONFERENCES, THE NATIONAL FOOTBALL CONFERENCE (NFC) AND THE AMERICAN FOOTBALL CONFERENCE (AFC) UNDER THE BANNER OF THE NFL. THE OLD AFL TEAMS STAYED TOGETHER IN THE AFC. THREE OLDER NFL FRANCHISES ALSO MOVED TO THE AFC SO THE CONFERENCES WOULD BE BALANCED.

But Namath was convinced his team was good enough to win. In fact, three days before the game, Namath told a crowd at the Miami Touchdown Club that his team would come out on top. "I guarantee it," he said.

That didn't make Jets coach Weeb Ewbank very happy, but Namath and his teammates felt they were every bit as good as the Colts. The Jets used a strong defense and the running of Matt Snell, who finished with 121 yards, to stun the football world. The Jets walked away with a 16-7 victory over Baltimore that showed that the AFL belonged. And that Broadway Joe knew what he was talking about.

GERRY PHILBIN SACKS QB JOHNNY UNITAS IN SUPER BOWL III.

Call Him "INCREDELMAN"

Nobody in the NFL seemed to care that Julian Edelman had been a star at Kent State University in Ohio. He had passed for 1,820 yards and 13 touchdowns and run for 1,370 yards and 13 scores in 2008. But he couldn't get invited to the NFL Combine, where the best college players went to be evaluated by coaches and general managers.

Edelman didn't pout. Instead, at his workout for professional scouts, he ran the short shuttle sprint faster than any of the guys at the Combine did. That speed — plus Edelman's toughness and desire — convinced New England to pick him in the 2009 draft. It didn't matter that he was one of the last five players chosen. Edelman was in the NFL.

EDELMAN'S SIDELINE GRAB

He wasn't going to play quarterback. The Patriots already had a pretty good one: Tom Brady. Edelman moved to receiver and caught 37 passes as a rookie. He didn't see much action in the passing game the next two seasons. But he established himself as one of the league's top kick and punt return men. After that, Edelman became a vital part of the Pats' offense. He caught 105 passes in 2013 and 92 the following season. His knowledge of the offense and how to get open made him one of the most reliable targets in the league.

EDELMAN SHOWED EVERYONE THAT IT ISN'T ALWAYS A GOOD IDEA TO LEAVE CERTAIN PEOPLE OFF THE INVITATION LIST.

EDELMAN ON THE BENCH

CHRIS HOGAN

FACT:
PATRIOTS RECEIVER CHRIS HOGAN WAS ALSO LARGELY UNNOTICED AFTER HIS COLLEGE YEARS. HOGAN PLAYED ONE SEASON OF COLLEGE FOOTBALL AT MONMOUTH UNIVERSITY IN NEW JERSEY. PREVIOUSLY HE HAD BEEN A LACROSSE PLAYER AT PENN STATE. IN THE PLAYOFFS AFTER THE 2016 SEASON, HOGAN SET A PATRIOTS PLAYOFF RECORD WHEN HE RACKED UP 180 YARDS ON NINE CATCHES AGAINST THE PITTSBURGH STEELERS.

From the HARDWOOD to the GRIDIRON

There may be no longer, crazier route to the NFL than the one Antonio Gates took. Gates went to five colleges and never played a down of football at any of them. He was a standout power forward for Kent State's basketball team. When scouts told him he was too small (6 feet 4 inches) to play that position in the National Basketball Association, Gates decided to try pro football.

NO NFL TEAM DRAFTED GATES.

He arranged a workout in San Diego, and the Chargers loved what they saw. They signed Gates as a tight end, and he was a starter by the end of his rookie season. Gates caught 24 passes in 2003 and 81 the year after that. By the end of the 2016 season, Gates had topped 70 receptions in a season six times. He has scored more than 10 touchdowns in a season four times.

ANTONIO GATES SHAKES OFF A DEFENDER WITH A STIFF-ARM.

Gates is an eight-time Pro Bowler who is third all time in catches by a tight end and second in career TDs scored by someone at his position. He is San Diego's all-time leader in passes caught, receiving yards, and TD catches. Most surprisingly, Gates showed that it's possible to move from being an excellent basketball player to an even bigger NFL star.

GATES DREAMED OF PLAYING PRO BASKETBALL. WHEN THAT SEEMED UNLIKELY, HIS AGENT ARRANGED A TRYOUT WITH THE CHARGERS.

JAMES HARRISON

FACT:

EVEN THOUGH JAMES HARRISON WAS A TOP FOOTBALL AND TRACK PERFORMER IN HIGH SCHOOL, HE DIDN'T GET ANY COLLEGE SCHOLARSHIP OFFERS. HE WALKED ON AT KENT STATE AND WAS A FIRST-TEAM ALL-CONFERENCE CHOICE AFTER RACKING UP 15 QUARTERBACK SACKS. NO NFL TEAM DRAFTED HARRISON. BUT THE PITTSBURGH STEELERS SIGNED HIM, AND HE PLAYED IN FIVE STRAIGHT PRO BOWLS, FROM 2007 TO 2011.

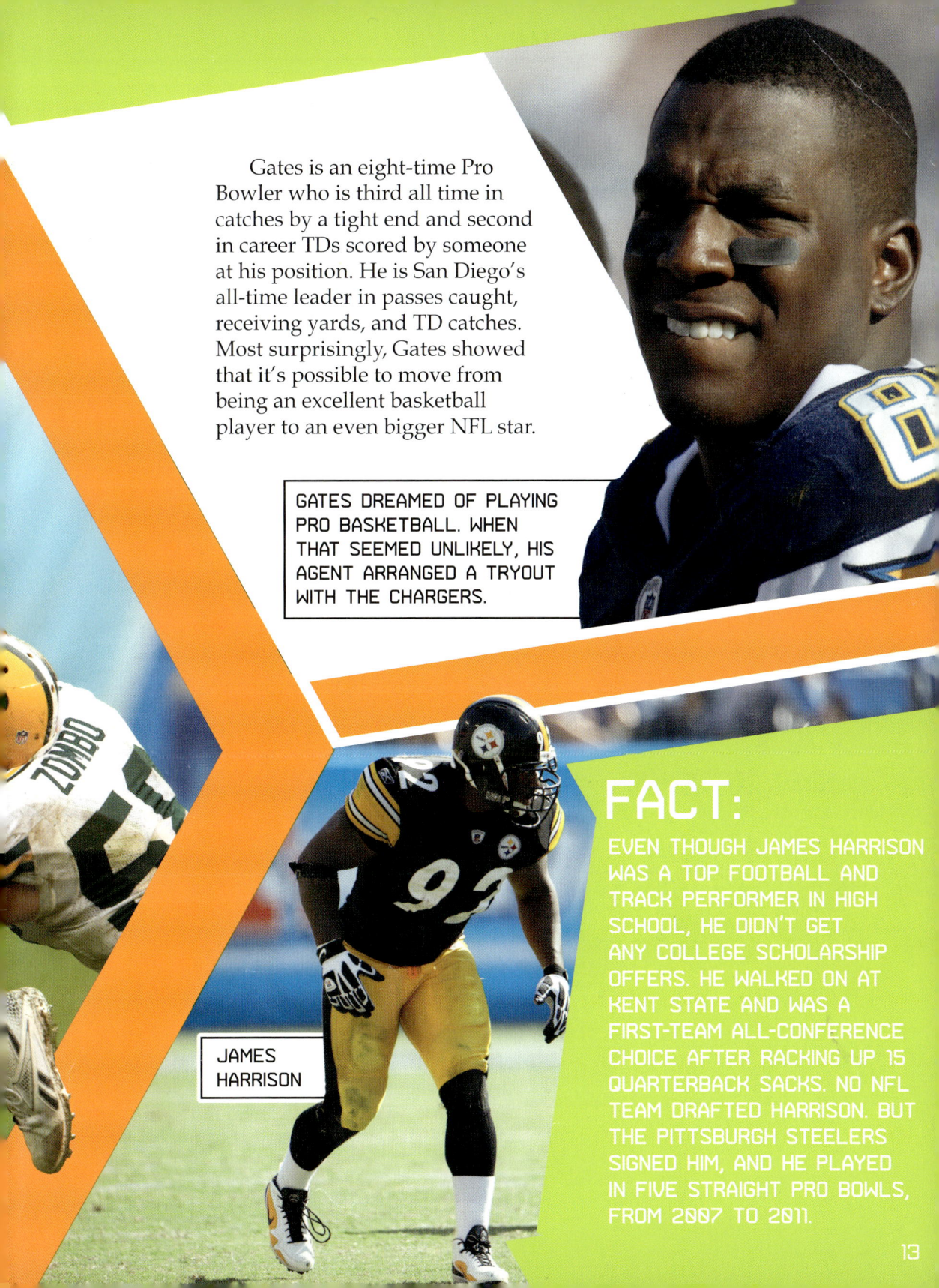

The Sneakers GAME

It may have been the most successful case of breaking and entering in football history. In 1934 the New York Giants faced the mighty Chicago Bears in the NFL championship game. The game was played on a frozen field at the Polo Grounds in New York. The Bears entered the game 13–0 and had won 18 straight, including the 1933 title game against the Giants.

Neither team could get any traction on the slick grass. The offenses struggled, but a Bronko Nagurski touchdown helped give the Bears a 10-3 halftime lead.

THE GIANTS AND BEARS PLAY IN THE NFL CHAMPIONSHIP GAME.

A BEARS PLAYER CHANGES FROM CLEATS TO GYM SHOES ON THE FROZEN FIELD.

While the Giants were sliding around on the frozen field, assistant clubhouse man Abe Cohen took action. Cohen, who also worked at nearby Manhattan College, used a hammer to break into the school's locker room. There, he found nine pairs of sneakers that he brought back to the stadium and gave to the New York players.

The rubber soles gripped the ground better than the players' metal cleats, and the Giants took over the game in the fourth quarter. They erased a 13-3 Chicago lead with two touchdown runs by powerful Ken Strong and the sharp passing of Ed Danowski.

Thanks to the sneakers, the Giants "skated" to a 30-13 victory. Their footwear helped them overcome the potent Bears and prove that sometimes underdogs need a little bit of extra help to claim victory.

FACT: BEARS PLAYER BRONKO NAGURSKI RANKS AS ONE OF COLLEGE AND PRO FOOTBALL'S GREATEST LEGENDS. LIKE MOST PLAYERS IN THAT ERA, HE PLAYED BOTH OFFENSE AND DEFENSE. ON OFFENSE, HE WAS A HUGE AND POWERFUL RUNNING BACK. ON DEFENSE, HE WAS A HARD-HITTING LINEMAN.

Ugly WINNERS

Just about everybody throughout the professional football world agreed: The 7-9 Seahawks didn't belong in the 2010 playoffs. And they certainly shouldn't have been hosting a game. But Seattle had won the NFC West Division. That meant a home game against the New Orleans Saints, the defending Super Bowl champions. While the media and fans screamed that the NFL should change its playoff format, Seattle prepared a big surprise.

The Seahawks were a 10-point underdog to Drew Brees and the Saints. Early on, it appeared as if New Orleans would have an easy time of it, holding leads of 10-0 and 17-7. But the quick start wasn't enough. The Saints had big problems in the kicking game and on defense. And even though their offense made seven trips inside the Seattle eight-yard line, they scored only four TDs.

QB MATT HASSELBECK

Meanwhile, Seahawks quarterback Matt Hasselbeck threw for 272 yards and four scores of his own. Three of them came to wide-open receivers as a result of the Saints' blown coverages.

Late in the fourth quarter, running back Marshawn Lynch went into full "Beast Mode." He plowed through just about the whole Saints defense on his way to a 67-yard TD. Seattle had a wild, 41-36 win, and all of those critics were pretty quiet.

MARSHAWN LYNCH

MARK VAN EEGHEN IN SUPER BOWL XV

FACT:

THE OAKLAND RAIDERS LOVED TO BE THE UNDERDOG. IN THE PLAYOFFS AFTER THE 1980 SEASON, THEY WHIPPED THE HOUSTON OILERS AT HOME. THEN THEY WON IN THE COLD AT CLEVELAND AND HELD OFF SAN DIEGO IN THE SUNSHINE TO REACH SUPER BOWL XV. AGAINST THE PHILADELPHIA EAGLES, OAKLAND INTERCEPTED THREE PASSES AND STIFLED THE EAGLES' OFFENSE IN A 27-10 WIN. THE RAIDERS BECAME THE FIRST WILD-CARD TEAM IN NFL HISTORY TO WIN THE SUPER BOWL.

Second Time's a CHARM

Before the Denver Broncos won their first championship, they had plenty of postseason disappointments. The Broncos suffered four losses in the Super Bowl and several other playoff setbacks. Few losses were as hard to handle as the 1996 divisional round loss to the Jacksonville Jaguars. The Jags were 14-point underdogs who were in just their second year in the NFL.

The Broncos had finished the season with the AFC's best record, 13–3, and won nine straight games during the heart of the season. The Jaguars, who were coached by Tom Coughlin, had posted a modest 9–7 record. They needed a wild-card win on the road at Buffalo to set up the meeting with Denver.

NATRONE MEANS LED THE JAGUARS' GROUND GAME.

THE JAGS' DEFENSE STUFFS DENVER'S JOHN ELWAY ON A QB SNEAK NEAR THE GOAL LINE.

The Broncos were looking ahead to an AFC matchup against New England and didn't consider the Jags much of a threat. That was a big mistake. Jacksonville used the powerful running of Natrone Means and Mark Brunell's strong arm to shock the Broncos. Means finished with 140 yards. Brunell threw for 245 yards and two TDs. The Jags won 30-27.

After the game, Denver tight end Shannon Sharpe said, "I'm just going to go home, sit on my couch, and probably cry." He wouldn't have been alone. Meanwhile, the Jaguars were delighted to contribute another chapter to the Broncos' sad postseason story.

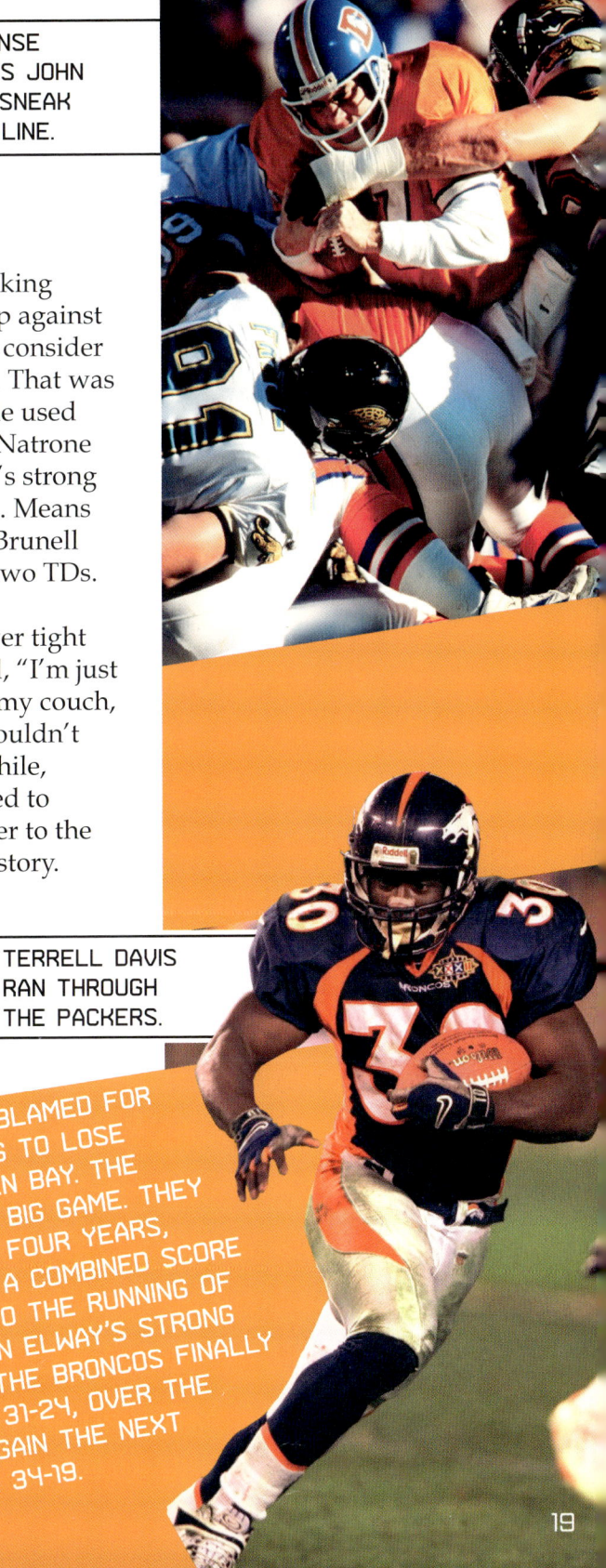

TERRELL DAVIS RAN THROUGH THE PACKERS.

FACT:
NOBODY COULD HAVE BEEN BLAMED FOR THINKING DENVER WAS GOING TO LOSE SUPER BOWL XXXII TO GREEN BAY. THE BRONCOS WERE 0-4 IN THE BIG GAME. THEY HAD LOST THREE TIMES IN FOUR YEARS, FROM 1987 TO 1990, WITH A COMBINED SCORE OF 136-40. BUT THANKS TO THE RUNNING OF TERRELL DAVIS, AND JOHN ELWAY'S STRONG PLAY AT QUARTERBACK, THE BRONCOS FINALLY GOT A SUPER BOWL WIN, 31-24, OVER THE PACKERS. THEY DID IT AGAIN THE NEXT YEAR, BEATING ATLANTA 34-19.

Sweet REVENGE

The rematch wasn't supposed to be much different from the first meeting. The Indianapolis Colts had crushed the Pittsburgh Steelers, 26-7, during the 2005 regular season. That victory helped the Colts post an NFL-best 14–2 record that featured a 13–0 start. A similar outcome was expected when the Steelers visited Indy for a divisional playoff game.

Pittsburgh had squeaked into the playoffs as the sixth seed, with an 11–5 record. They needed to beat the Cincinnati Bengals on the road to earn a rematch with the Colts.

The Colts were a team to be feared. Indy quarterback Peyton Manning was once again outstanding, and running back Edgerrin James was one of the NFL's best. That's why so many people were stunned when the Steelers held a 21-3 lead heading into the fourth quarter.

RECEIVER HINES WARD LED THE UNDERDOG STEELERS.

FACT: THE STEELERS ADVANCED TO THE SUPER BOWL AFTER UPSETTING THE COLTS. IN SUPER BOWL XL, PLAYED IN DETROIT IN EARLY 2006, THE STEELERS KNOCKED OFF THE SEATTLE SEAHAWKS.

Pittsburgh almost gave everything away in the final 15 minutes. Manning led a pair of touchdown drives to cut the lead to 21-18 with less than five minutes remaining. It wasn't until the Colts missed a tying field goal in the final seconds that the Steelers could celebrate. "Nobody said we could win," Pittsburgh receiver Hines Ward said after the game. He was right.

AND EVERYBODY HAD BEEN WRONG.

TROY POLAMALU (43) PICKED OFF A PASS, BUT THE OFFICIALS REVERSED THE CALL IN ERROR. STILL, THE STEELERS HELD ON.

ANTWAAN RANDLE EL

21

JOHNNY U.

Fans who turned out in Pittsburgh to watch the Bloomfield Rams during the semi-pro team's 1955 season had no idea they were seeing a legend in the making. The man playing quarterback, safety, and punter for Bloomfield would end up being one of the greatest players in NFL history.

Johnny Unitas had been drafted in 1955 by the Steelers, his hometown team. But coach Walt Kiesling didn't think the hometown hero was smart enough to play QB. The coach cut him. Unitas worked construction to support his family and played for Bloomfield. The next season, he gave the NFL another try, this time with the Baltimore Colts.

JOHNNY UNITAS

JOHNNY UNITAS PASSING IN A GAME AGAINST THE LOS ANGELES RAMS

You might say it worked out pretty well. After establishing himself as a starter during his rookie season in 1956, Unitas became the best quarterback in the NFL. During the next four years, Unitas topped the league in touchdown passes each season and in passing yards three times. He did that while leading the Colts to NFL championships in 1958 and 1959.

During his long career, Unitas was named the league's most valuable player (MVP) four times. He also invented the two-minute drill. Working without a huddle, he would call plays at the line of scrimmage and hurry his team down field to get a late-game score as time ran down. As a result, Unitas led the NFL in fourth-quarter comebacks seven times. For a guy who wasn't good enough or smart enough to handle the position, Unitas certainly did well.

And he gave those semi-pro fans a chance to say they saw him before he was known far and wide as "Johnny U."

FACT: BLOOMFIELD IS A NEIGHBORHOOD IN PITTSBURGH, AND THE RAMS WERE PART OF A SEMI-PRO LEAGUE THAT FOLDED LONG AGO. UNITAS RECEIVED $6 PER GAME DURING HIS ONE SEASON WITH THE RAMS. HE TOOK OVER AS STARTING QUARTERBACK AFTER SHOWING HIMSELF TO BE A BETTER PASSER THAN CHARLES "BEAR" RODGERS, WHO WAS THE TEAM'S PLAYER-COACH.

Supermarket to SUPER BOWL

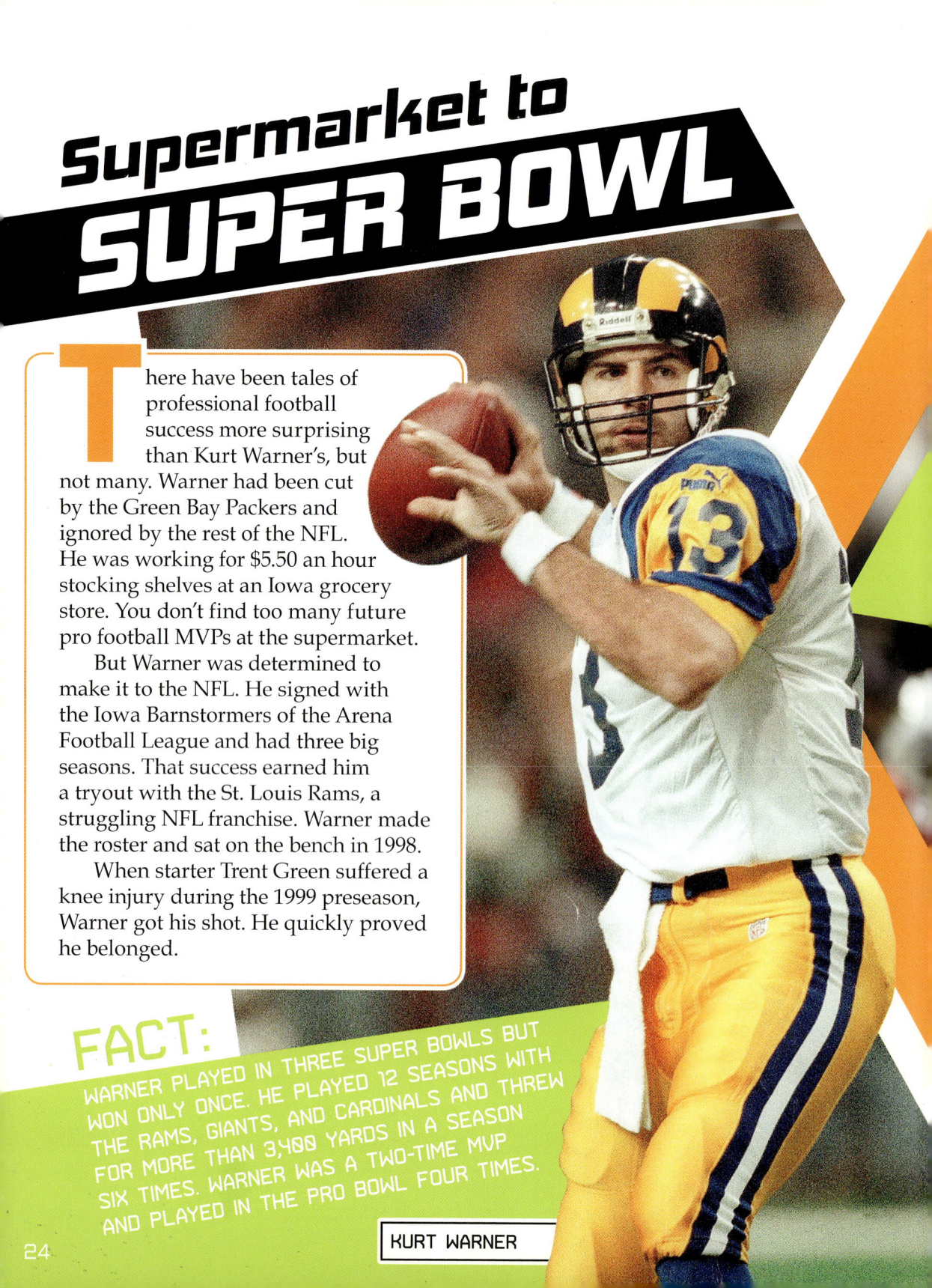

There have been tales of professional football success more surprising than Kurt Warner's, but not many. Warner had been cut by the Green Bay Packers and ignored by the rest of the NFL. He was working for $5.50 an hour stocking shelves at an Iowa grocery store. You don't find too many future pro football MVPs at the supermarket.

But Warner was determined to make it to the NFL. He signed with the Iowa Barnstormers of the Arena Football League and had three big seasons. That success earned him a tryout with the St. Louis Rams, a struggling NFL franchise. Warner made the roster and sat on the bench in 1998.

When starter Trent Green suffered a knee injury during the 1999 preseason, Warner got his shot. He quickly proved he belonged.

FACT:
WARNER PLAYED IN THREE SUPER BOWLS BUT WON ONLY ONCE. HE PLAYED 12 SEASONS WITH THE RAMS, GIANTS, AND CARDINALS AND THREW FOR MORE THAN 3,400 YARDS IN A SEASON SIX TIMES. WARNER WAS A TWO-TIME MVP AND PLAYED IN THE PRO BOWL FOUR TIMES.

KURT WARNER

Warner led the NFL with 41 touchdowns that season. He completed a league-leading 65.1 percent of his passes and helped St. Louis to a 13-3 record, tops in the NFC. Then he led the Rams to Super Bowl XXXIV and racked up 414 passing yards and two TDs in the title game. After guiding the Rams to a 23-16 win over the Tennessee Titans, Warner was named the Super Bowl MVP.

LATE IN HIS CAREER, WARNER LED THE CARDS TO THE SUPER BOWL.

Nine years later, he was back in the big game, this time with the Arizona Cardinals. Although he didn't come out on top, Warner again finished with impressive numbers. It was another amazing chapter in a story that remains one of the most improbable in NFL history.

25

The AFTERTHOUGHT

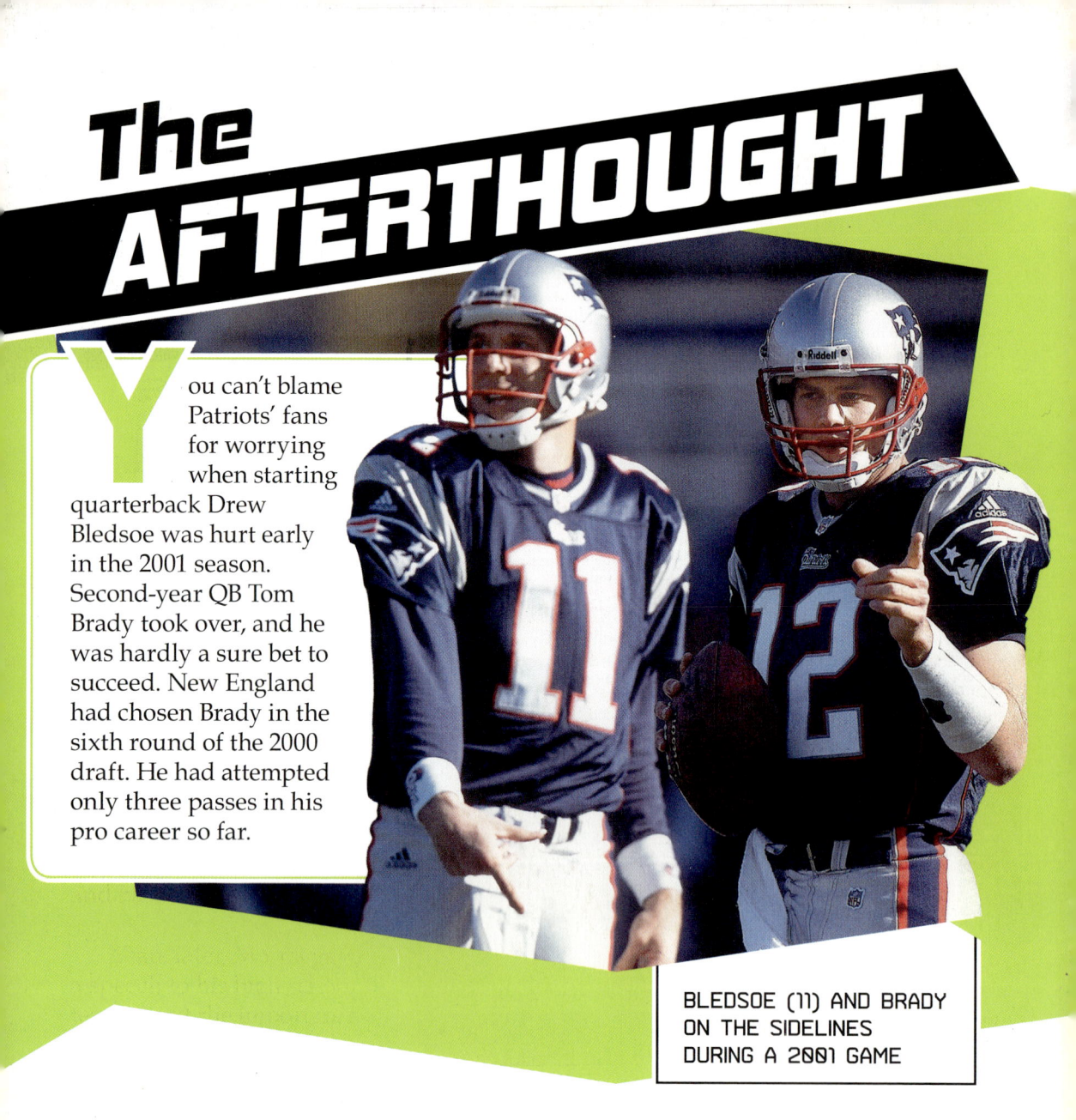

You can't blame Patriots' fans for worrying when starting quarterback Drew Bledsoe was hurt early in the 2001 season. Second-year QB Tom Brady took over, and he was hardly a sure bet to succeed. New England had chosen Brady in the sixth round of the 2000 draft. He had attempted only three passes in his pro career so far.

BLEDSOE (11) AND BRADY ON THE SIDELINES DURING A 2001 GAME

Brady had been the sixth quarterback selected in 2000, behind forgettable signal-callers such as Giovanni Carmozzi and Spergon Wynn. Still, he led that Patriots team all the way to Super Bowl XXXVI. There, he threw for a touchdown and was named MVP of the Patriots' surprising 20-17 win over the St. Louis Rams.

FROM THERE, BRADY BLOSSOMED INTO ONE OF THE GREATEST QUARTERBACKS OF ALL TIME.

He is a two-time NFL MVP who has led the Pats to five Super Bowl titles. In four seasons he has topped the league in TD passes. He has also led the NFL in passing yards twice. His best performance came in 2007, when he threw 50 touchdown passes and only eight interceptions while completing a career-best 68.9 percent of his passes for 4,806 yards.

As it turned out, the man only the Patriots wanted became somebody every NFL team would have loved to have.

FACT:
EVEN THOUGH TONY ROMO WON THE 2002 WALTER PAYTON AWARD AS THE TOP FOOTBALL CHAMPIONSHIP SUBDIVISION (FCS) PLAYER, NO NFL TEAM WAS IMPRESSED ENOUGH TO DRAFT HIM. (FCS COLLEGES ARE ONE LEVEL DOWN FROM THE BIG TIME IN DIVISION I.) ROMO SIGNED WITH THE DALLAS COWBOYS AS A FREE AGENT. AFTER TWO SEASONS, HE TOOK OVER AS STARTING QUARTERBACK. HE BECAME A STAR AND PLAYED IN FOUR PRO BOWLS.

Ending an ERA in STYLE

It would be the last game involving a team from the American Football League. When Super Bowl IV was over, the AFL and NFL would merge to become one happy group of football teams. The leagues had already been drafting college players together. In 1970 they would join forces completely.

But Kansas City wanted to make sure the AFL would be remembered as a championship league forever. One year after the New York Jets pulled off a momentous upset over Baltimore in the Super Bowl, the Chiefs were two-touchdown underdogs. They were expected to be shut down by the fearsome Vikings, much like they had been by Green Bay three years earlier in Super Bowl I.

CHIEFS COACH HANK STRAM WAS CARRIED OFF THE FIELD IN CELEBRATION OF THE UPSET.

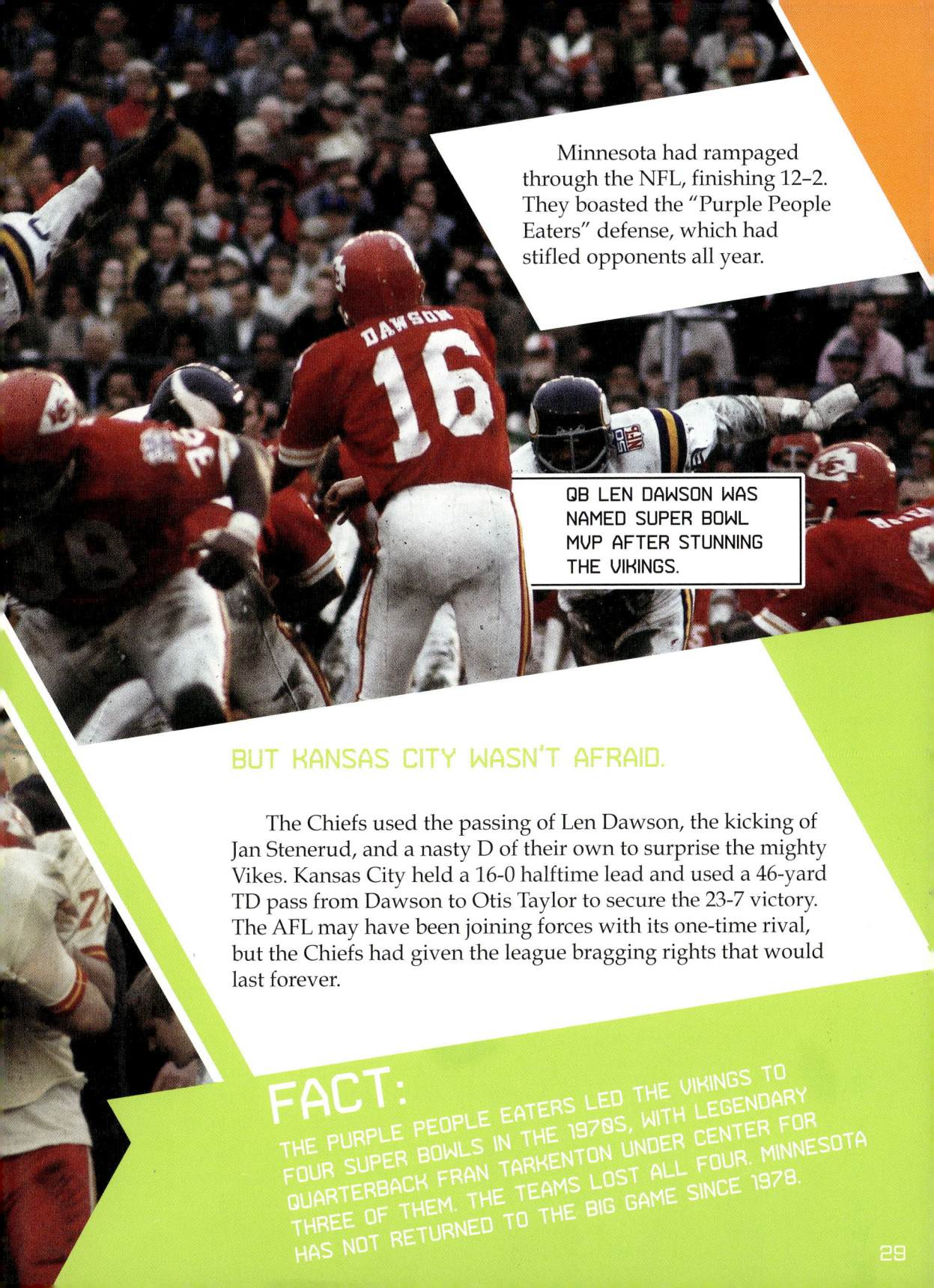

Minnesota had rampaged through the NFL, finishing 12–2. They boasted the "Purple People Eaters" defense, which had stifled opponents all year.

QB LEN DAWSON WAS NAMED SUPER BOWL MVP AFTER STUNNING THE VIKINGS.

BUT KANSAS CITY WASN'T AFRAID.

The Chiefs used the passing of Len Dawson, the kicking of Jan Stenerud, and a nasty D of their own to surprise the mighty Vikes. Kansas City held a 16-0 halftime lead and used a 46-yard TD pass from Dawson to Otis Taylor to secure the 23-7 victory. The AFL may have been joining forces with its one-time rival, but the Chiefs had given the league bragging rights that would last forever.

FACT:
THE PURPLE PEOPLE EATERS LED THE VIKINGS TO FOUR SUPER BOWLS IN THE 1970S, WITH LEGENDARY QUARTERBACK FRAN TARKENTON UNDER CENTER FOR THREE OF THEM. THE TEAMS LOST ALL FOUR. MINNESOTA HAS NOT RETURNED TO THE BIG GAME SINCE 1978.

Underdog ROUNDUP

Centre College (1921): Mighty Harvard had not lost a game in nearly five years when Centre College visited Boston in October 1921. The tiny school from Danville, Kentucky, had dropped a 31-14 decision to the Harvard Crimson a season earlier and wasn't given much of a chance. The teams were tied 0-0 at the half, but a touchdown by Bo McMillan gave Centre a 6-0 lead that it didn't surrender. The "Praying Colonels," who had prayed at halftime of a previous game, pulled off one of the biggest upsets in college football history. Back home, fans painted "C6H0" (Centre 6, Harvard 0) all over town.

Timmy Smith: This rookie had only carried the ball in four games during the 1987 regular season. But when the playoffs came around, Washington coach Joe Gibbs gave the fifth-round pick the ball. Smith gained 66 and 72 yards in two Redskins victories. He was better in the Super Bowl, gaining a record 204 yards and scoring twice in a 42-10 rout over the Denver Broncos.

Dexter Jackson: A fourth-round draft pick, Jackson had been a steady performer in Tampa Bay's secondary. But in Super Bowl XXXVII, the four-year veteran turned into a superhero. Jackson intercepted two passes and was named the MVP of the Buccaneers' 48-21 win over the Oakland Raiders.

Appalachian State: More than 110,000 people packed Michigan Stadium for the opening game of their Wolverines' 2007 season. It's a safe bet many fans didn't even know where Appalachian State was located. (It's in Boone, N.C.) The Mountaineers were supposed to provide a tune-up for fifth-ranked University of Michigan. Even though Appalachian State was ranked first in the FCS poll, a team from a lower division was not expected to pose a threat. Surprise! Michigan held a slim, 32-31 lead with 4:26 remaining. Appalachian State drilled a 24-yard field goal with 26 seconds left to make it 34-32. Then they blocked a Michigan field goal attempt on the last play, giving the Mountaineers one of the biggest upsets in sports history.

READ MORE

Doeden, Matt. *Fantasy Football Math.* North Mankato, Minn.: Capstone Press, 2016.

The Editors of Sports Illustrated Kids. *The Big Book of Who Football.* New York: Sports Illustrated, 2015.

Hetrick, Hans. *Football's Record Breakers.* North Mankato, Minn.: Capstone Press, 2017.

INTERNET SITES

Use FactHound to find Internet sites related to this book.

Visit www.facthound.com

Just type in 9781515780489 and go.

INDEX

Appalachian State, 31
Arizona Cardinals, 24, 25

Baltimore Colts, 8-9, 22-23
Bledsoe, Drew, 26
Bloomfield Rams, 22, 23
Brady, Tom, 4, 11, 26-27
Brunell, Mark, 19

Centre College, 30
Chicago Bears, 14-15

Dallas Cowboys, 4, 27
Davis, Terrell, 19
Dawson, Len, 29
Denver Broncos, 18-19, 30

Edelman, Julian, 10-11
Ewbank, Weeb, 9

Gates, Antonio, 12-13
Green Bay Packers, 8, 19, 24

Harrison, James, 13
Harvard, 30
Hasselbeck, Matt, 16, 17
Hogan, Chris, 11

Indianapolis Colts, 20-21

Jackson, Dexter, 31
Jacksonville Jaguars, 18-19

Kansas City Chiefs, 8, 28-29

Lynch, Marshawn, 17

Manning, Eli, 4-5, 6-7
Manning, Peyton, 20-21
Means, Natrone, 18, 19
Miami Dolphins, 6-7
Minnesota Vikings, 28-29

Nagurski, Bronko, 14, 15
Namath, Joe, 8-9
New England Patriots, 4-5, 6-7, 10-11, 26-27
New Orleans Saints, 16-17
New York Giants, 4-5, 6-7, 14-15, 24
New York Jets, 8-9, 28

Oakland Raiders, 8, 17, 31

Pittsburgh Steelers, 11, 13, 20-21, 22

Romo, Tony, 27

San Diego Chargers, 12-13, 17
Seattle Seahawks, 16-17, 21
Sharpe, Shannon, 19
Smith, Timmy, 30
St. Louis Rams, 24-25, 26

Tampa Bay Buccaneers, 31
Tarkenton, Fran, 29
Tyree, David, 5, 7

Unitas, Johnny, 9, 22-23
University of Michigan, 31

Ward, Hines, 20, 21
Warner, Kurt, 24-25
Washington Redskins, 7, 30